Rescue Machines At Work

Fire Engines

By E.S. Budd

The Child's World, Inc. ◆ Eden Prairie, Minnesota

Published by The Child's World®, Inc.
7081 W. 192 Ave.
Eden Prairie, MN 55346

Design and Production:
The Creative Spark, San Juan Capistrano, CA

Photos: © 1998 David M. Budd Photography

Library of Congress Cataloging-in-Publication Data

Budd, E. S.
     Fire engines / by E. S. Budd
        p. cm.
     Includes index.
     Summary: A simple description of fire engines, what they do, and
how they work.
     ISBN 1-56766-656-6 (lib. bdg. : alk. paper)
     1. Fire engines—Juvenile literature. 2. Fire extinction—Juvenile
literature. [1. Fire engines. 2. Fire fighters.] I. Title.
TH9372.B84 1999
628.9'259—dc21
                                      99-28598
                                           CIP

Contents

On the Job   4

Climb Aboard!   18

Up Close   20

Glossary   24

On the Job

On the job, a fire engine helps put out fires. A fire engine carries big **hoses.**

4

Fire fighters attach one end of a hose to a **fire hydrant.** The hydrant is like a big pipe. It gets water from the town's supply. The fire fighters attach the other end of the hose to the engine's **pump.**

The pump can carry water to a **nozzle** on top of the truck. The fire fighters use the nozzle to spray water at the fire.

Fire engines carry many important tools. Some tools help fire fighters rescue people. Other tools help them put out fires. Tools are kept in **bins.**

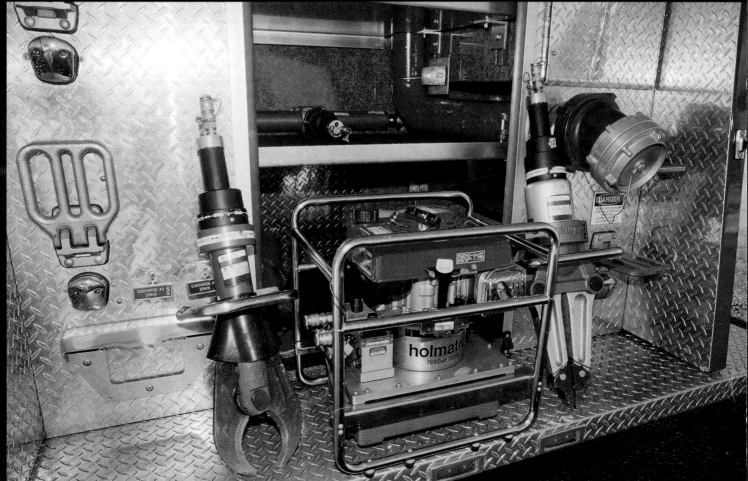

Fire engines have bright lights.

They warn other drivers that the

engine is moving fast.

The fire engine also has **sirens** and

noisy horns. They are very loud!

The engine is kept at the fire station.

It is always ready to go in an emergency.

Climb Aboard!

Would you like to see where the fire fighters sit? The driver is called an **engineer.** Other fire fighters sit in the back. It is very loud inside the truck. All the firemen wear headphones to talk to each other. The engineer also has a **radio.** He uses it to talk to people at the fire station.

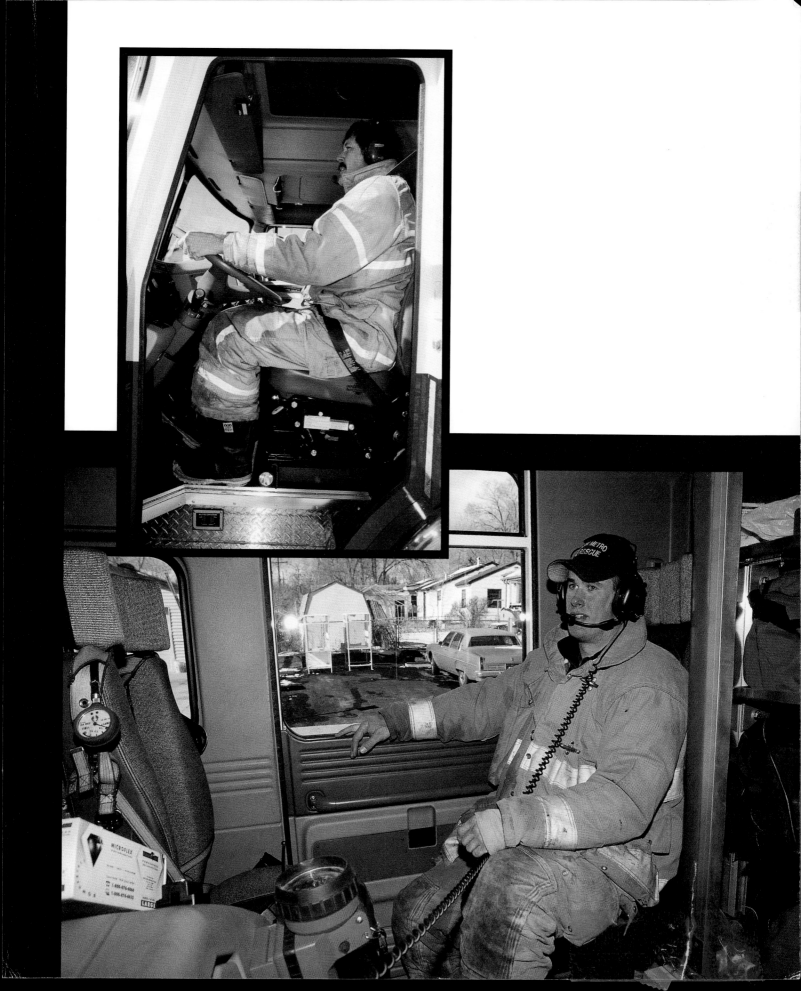

Up Close

The inside

1. The headphones

2. The steering wheel

3. The radio

The outside

1. The pump

2. The hose

3. The lights

4. The sirens

5. The tool bins

Glossary

bins (BINZ)
Bins are boxes inside the fire engine. The fire fighters store tools inside the bins.

fire hydrant (FY-er HY-drent)
A fire hydrant is a pipe with a big spout. Fire fighters use the engine to pump water from a hydrant.

engineer (en-je-NEER)
An engineer is the driver of a fire truck. He or she sits in the front of the truck.

hoses (HOH-zez)
Hoses are long tubes that can move something wet. A fire fighter attaches hoses to fire hydrants.

nozzle (NAWZ-el)
A nozzle is a tool attached to a hose or a pump. It helps spray water in the right direction.

pump (PUMP)
A pump is a device that lifts and moves something wet. Fire fighters use pumps to get water from hydrants.

radio (RAYD-ee-o)
A radio is a special machine on a fire engine. The engineer uses the radio to talk to people at the fire station.

sirens (SY-renz)
Sirens are horns that make very loud noises. A fire engine has sirens to warn people it is coming.

4/03

ML